Start-Off Stories

THREE BILLY GOATS GRUFF

Retold by Patricia and Fredrick McKissack

Illustrated by Tom Dunnington

Prepared under the direction of Robert Hillerich, Ph.D.

CHILDRENS PRESS®

CHICAGO

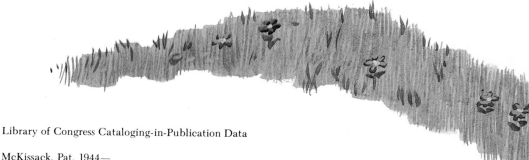

Library of Congress Cataloging-in-Publication Data

McKissack, Pat, 1944—
   Three billy goats gruff.

   (Start-off stories)
   Summary: An easy-to-read retelling of the fairy tale
about three clever goats and a nasty troll.
   [1. Fairy tales. 2. Folklore—Norway] I. McKissack,
Fredrick. II. Dunnington, Tom, ill. III. Asbjornsen,
Peter Christen, 1812-1885. Tre bukkene Bruse.
IV. Title. V. Title: 3 billy goats gruff. VI. Series.
PZ8.1.M463Ti   1987   398.2'4529735809481 [E]   86-33450
ISBN 0-516-02366-7

One.
Two.
Three.
Three billy goats named Gruff.

Little Billy Goat Gruff.
Big Billy Goat Gruff.

Very Big Billy Goat Gruff.

They eat here.
But, they want to eat there.

"Let us go over there to eat,"
says Very Big Billy Goat Gruff.

"I will go over,"
says Little Billy Goat Gruff.

Tip tap, tip tap, tip tap.

10

"Who is that over me?"
says the Troll.
"I will eat you!"

"No. Let me go. I am little.
Big Billy Goat Gruff will
be better to eat."

13

So, Little Billy Goat Gruff goes back.

"I will go over,"
says Big Billy Goat Gruff.

Bump thump, bump thump, bump thump.

"Who is that over me?"
says the Troll.
"I will eat you!"

"No. No. Let me go.
Very Big Billy Goat Gruff
will be better to eat."

So, Big Billy Goat Gruff goes back.

"I will go over,"
says Very Big Billy Goat Gruff.

RUMP-RUMP-RUMP-
RUMP-RUMP.

"Who is that over me?"
says the Troll.
"I will eat you!"

"No you will not!"
says Very Big Billy Goat Gruff.
"I will stop you!"

24

And, he did.
Bam!
Slam!
SPLASH!

So, the Little Billy Goat Gruff
goes over.

The Big Billy Goat Gruff
goes over.

The Very Big Billy Goat Gruff
goes over.

One.
Two.
Three.
Three Billy Goats named Gruff.
They eat here. They eat there.
They eat anywhere.

WORD LIST

am	Gruff	splash
and	he	tap
anywhere	here	that
back	I	the
bam	is	there
be	let	they
better	little	three
big	me	thump
billy	named	tip
bump	no	to
but	not	troll
did	one	two
eat	over	us
go	rump	very
goat	says	want
goats	slam	who
goes	so	will
	stop	you

The vocabulary of *Three Billy Goats Gruff* correlates with the following lists:
Dolch 75%, Hillerich 71%, Durr 71%

About the Authors

Patricia and Fredrick McKissack are freelance writers, editors, and teachers of writing. They are the owners of All-Writing Services, located in Clayton, Missouri. Since 1975, the McKissacks have published numerous magazine articles and stories for juvenile and adult readers. They also have conducted educational and editorial workshops throughout the country. The McKissacks and their three teenage sons live in a large remodeled inner-city home in St. Louis.

About the Artist

Tom Dunnington hails from the Midwest, having lived in Minnesota, Iowa, Illinois, and Indiana. He attended the John Herron Institute of Art in Indianapolis and the American Academy of Art and the Chicago Art Institute in Chicago. He has been an art instructor and illustrator for many years. In addition to illustrating books, Mr. Dunnington is working on a series of paintings of endangered birds (produced as limited edition prints). His current residence is in Oak Park, Illinois, where he works as a free-lance illustrator and is active in church and community youth work.